UNLOCKING LOVE

The Key to Changing Two Lives

DANA ROEHRIG & DE DE COX

Copyright © 2023 by Dana Roehrig & de de Cox

UNLOCKING LOVE

All rights reserved. No part of this publication may be reproduced, distributed, or transmitted in any form or by any means, including photocopying, recording, or other electronic or mechanical methods, without the prior written permission of the publisher, except in the case of brief quotations embodied in critical reviews and certain other noncommercial uses permitted by copyright law. For permission requests, write to the publisher, addressed "Attention: Permissions Coordinator," at info@beyondpublishing.net

Female Model:	Savannah Dean Reeves
Male Model:	Bo Cox
Photography:	Austin Ozier / Medici Creative
HMUA:	Scooter Minyard
HMUA Assistant:	Jeanette Moore
Wardrobe:	Andre Wilson / Style Icon, LLC
Caterer:	Carol DeSoto / Subway
Location:	Crowne Plaza, Louisville, KY

Quantity sales and special discounts are available on quantity purchases by corporations, associations, and others. For details, contact the publisher at the address above. Orders by U.S. trade bookstores and wholesalers. Email info@BeyondPublishing.net

The Beyond Publishing Speakers Bureau can bring authors to your live event. For more information or to book an event contact the Beyond Publishing Speakers Bureau speak@BeyondPublishing.net

The Author can be reached directly at BeyondPublishing.net
Manufactured and printed in the United States of America distributed globally by BeyondPublishing.net

New York | Los Angeles | London | Sydney

ISBN Hardcover:
ISBN Softcover:

DEDICATION

Carol DeSoto

In life, how many true friends can you count? Not many. You know what I am talking about. Those friends you know right after meeting them they are going to become a part of your life. This is Carol DeSoto. Watching her that one day while I stood in line to get lunch, I listened as she spoke to all her customers with such kind words and asking questions about their family and how the weekend was. I knew she and I would immediately hit it off. We began talking in line as she was completing my order and before you know it, I had invited her to my book signing. Now to be honest, I did not think she would come because I knew how busy she was. She was running and is still running her own store, which has been and continues to be very successful. We are now going on five years of friendship. Carol is now the official sponsor caterer of all my photoshoots. There are not enough words to say how much her kindness means to me to share her time and to be a part of something that she knows means the world to me. God always places people in our life sometimes for a few seconds, a few days, a few months, and then HE places those like Carol in your life forever. I'm grateful that HE knew I needed Carol. She truly represents Acts 20:35.

PROLOGUE

The incessant ringing. What was it? It would not stop. It dawned on her it was her cell phone that somehow had found its way onto the floor under her bed. She rolled over with her eyes half-shut, half-open. Trying her best to maintain her balance, she peered at the alarm clock. Her eyes were still clouded with sleep. It was 2:00 a.m. Who in the world would be calling at 2:00 a.m.? She inched her way to the side of the mattress, while trying to balance and not fall off. She peered underneath. She could see the light blinking on and off from the ringing sound. She reached for her cell and saw it was a number she did not recognize. Typically, she would just ignore a number she did not recognize. But it was 2:00 a.m. Call it intuition, she knew she needed to answer. Her voice was still groggy from sleep. "Hello, hello, who is this?" She heard the words "Ms. Griffin, it's Dixon Memorial Hospital. Your parents have been in a motor vehicle accident."

She jumped up at the word "accident." She told the hospital receptionist that she would book a flight as quickly as possible. She should arrive within four to five hours. She asked, "Are my parents okay?" The hospital receptionist would only say that both were stable at this time. She was up and packing her bags before she could end the conversation.

****

This meeting needed to take place. It had been long overdue. It was time to make the move into the industry. The company's future depended on him, as well as the family's. There was no room for mistakes. Both companies needed each other. It was a win-win-situation. It was up to him to convince both sides that it was the perfect marriage.

In business, this was true. In his life, not so much so. He had no time for a personal relationship. The only interest he had was the completion of the merger into one. He looked at the briefcase he was holding that contained the documents that would combine two into one.

He smirked. Unfortunately, that did sound a bit like marriage. The documents were signed, sealed, notarized and ready for recording. Now just to return home and begin his future.

CHAPTER 1

The cab dropped her off. The last few months had been a blur. The funeral. The withdrawal from college. Camryn had left the attorney's office earlier than anticipated. All she wanted to do was get to the airport, check her bag in, sit down and wait. She needed time to take it all in. The meeting with Mr. Laurence Fine did not last long. He explained how an estate would need to be opened to handle the assets and distribution of property of Mom and Pop Pop. Mr. Fine had told her she was the sole heir of their estate. Camryn had signed documents that would allow Mr. Fine to handle everything on her behalf without her having to fly back. The rest of the paperwork could be done via email. She could not believe how tired she was. The airport check-in was easy. Camryn held on to the briefcase as if her life depended on it. Mr. Fine told her he did not have time to go over a full explanation of the contents, but when she returned home, to call him and set a teleconference appointment. He would explain everything inside.

The airline attendant had announced to the passengers still remaining that the flight was full and the wait time would be thirty to forty-five minutes before boarding would begin.

The only thing left to do was sit and wait for the boarding announcement. She found a seat against the window. Camryn laid her head back and looked up to the ceiling. She had time. Should she open the briefcase and peek inside? She reached into her purse. Camryn placed her hand on it. It was there. The key. It was still cold to her touch. Nothing had changed since the morning meeting with Mr. Fine and his delivery of the briefcase and key. She had no idea the contents of the briefcase. Instinct told her it would be best not to disagree with Mr. Fine while in his office. She recalled his placement of the key into the palm of her hand this morning. A shiver ran up her spine, even though she was sitting in the warm window at the airport. This tiny innate object would unlock specific instructions for her moving forward without Mom and Pop Pop. There was no way she could not be curious. Mr. Fine was being tight-lipped. He had placed his business card in her hand. Mr. Fine reiterated the follow up call that would need to be made. She could not argue with him. Everything was moving at lightning speed.

Still clutching the key inside her purse, her eyes closed.

CHAPTER 2

Finally, the meeting adjourned.

Barrett Drew was free from all their questions, their concerns, their comments, their conversation of chit-chat that was going nowhere but wasting his time.

Being the president of Vegas Heat for five years, a digital consulting firm, founded by husband and wife Lily and Everett Dean, most underestimated his knowledge and understanding of the digital market. The Dean family had allowed him leeway with decisions for the firm's growth. Barrett had been placed in their circle of trust, whether he wanted it or not.

He knew that the Dean family had no idea how quickly the firm would expand, especially with this specific merger.

Everything and everyone were moving to the digital world, especially when it came to marketing their brand.

Vegas Heat had climbed into the top ten of digital consulting firms within less than six months. This was unheard of. They had only been on the exchange for less than two months.

The motivation and commitment to be number one was dependent on the meeting with Dynamic Connections. Lily and Everett Dean had instructed him to call so that they could discuss the meeting's outcome.

The meeting had ended as Barrett expected. All agreed that Dynamic Connections would merge with Vegas Heat.

CHAPTER 3

There was little travel time remaining. Barrett had done pre-registration for the flight. He needed to get to the airport in record time. Otherwise, kiss the flight goodbye. Standing on the street corner, Barrett saw the Uber turn the corner. He had not placed the briefcase down since leaving Dynamic's offices. Even though the documents would be scanned before Barrett arrived home, there was always a chance of a glitch in the scanning or in the forwarding of the documents via email. The briefcase held all the original signed merger-and-acquisition documents. There was nothing more secure than having the originals in your possession.

The storm had emerged from nowhere. The weather service had issued a severe thunderstorm warning with possible tornado formation. Sitting in the airport waiting for the flights to be called and watching the time delays was annoying. He got up from the chair and walked to where the flight attendant was speaking with several other attendants. This could not be good news. Barrett could tell by their facial features, plus the fact they were whispering and looking at the individuals seated for the flights. That was a dead giveaway that the news was not going to be positive. Before he could inquire, the attendant came across the speaker with the announcement that the flights had been cancelled and would be rescheduled in the morning.

In addition, Southeastern Airlines would pay for hotel accommodations for those individuals affected. Reservations were being made at Dearing Hotel Suites. Shuttles would transport to and from the airport. It was made clear that the airline attendants would see everyone in the morning at 6:00 a.m. to begin their next day air travels.

Had long had she dozed off? Camryn was exhausted physically, but more so mentally. Home. She needed to get home. Her ears perked as she heard the intercom system. All she heard was cancelled and rescheduled. Camryn knew she would need to go inquire as to what was going on. Sitting in the window, she had observed the lightning stretch across the sky. Based on the last twenty-four hours, it was inevitable that something would go wrong.

Rising, she saw several others waiting in line to speak to the attendant. Camryn could overhear the attendant begin the explanation. "Yes, yes, the airline would take care of the hotel expense for one night. Most flights were being rescheduled to 6:00 a.m., which meant an arrival time back at the airport at 4:00 a.m." The attendant smiled as he repeated the information about the shuttle service and then began the conversation with the next individual. Camryn laughed. No telling how many times this would be repeated before the evening ended.

CHAPTER 4

Walking through the airport, the briefcase had become heavy on her hand. Camryn had been informed there was only paperwork inside. No valuables. Nothing heavy. And yet, it seemed liked the world had been placed inside and locked away. Camryn's shoulders felt heavy carrying it. Her heart felt heavy, too. What secrets were in this briefcase? No matter what was found, she would never be able to ask Mom and Pop Pop about the contents.

Making her way to where the shuttle service was waiting, she was lost in thought. Camryn did not see him. Where did he come from? She could not stop herself. She bumped the cheek of his butt with her briefcase. Camryn stepped back.

Barrett turned around. The look in his eyes was irritating. She could tell he was not mad, but more annoyed than anything. His first words were meant to sting. Camryn could tell by the smirk of his lips. "In a hurry, are you? You are not going to get there any faster than the rest of us."

Camryn was going to apologize, but after that look of disdain from this stranger, there was no way in hell that was going to happen.

"Just like everyone else, sir, I am ready to get to the assigned hotel. I can assure you that bumping into you again will not happen." Barret stepped to the side to see if there was more than one shuttle approaching the passengers.

"Again, you are stuck, just like everyone else. Waiting. There is nothing more than to stand here. I suggest you get back behind me, as you were before."

"I'm sorry, what is your name, please?" she inquired.

"Oh, you are going to apologize. I appreciate you…"

Camryn cut him off. "Oh, no, I'm not apologize for bumping you, I'm excusing myself because I don't know what to call you. I'm just asking for your name. Please don't confuse the two."

Barrett could not stop. He smiled. He could not keep it in any longer. Barrett needed to be in a room all by himself and here he was arguing with a spitfire of all of about 64 inches.

Several of the passengers were smiling as well. Everyone was approaching "the giddy phase" from waiting so long at the airport. One man elbowed him and said, "Just give in. It will make your life easier. Trust me. I've been married thirty-eight years, and whatever she says, I agree with." He winked at his wife.

Barrett busted out laughing. "Oh, we are definitely not married. I do not even know her name, but from those beautiful dark blue eyes darting daggers at me, I don't know that I need to poke the bear any more."

"Am I invisible? Standing right here. In front of both of you, as if you did not see me. I hear every word, especially the reference that I am a bear. Gentlemen, please let me reassure you that if you 'poke the bear,' there is no poking in return. You become fair game as a meal." Camryn placed her hands on her hips for punctuation.

The older gentleman smiled. "Not only are your hands going to be full, but I suspect your life is about to change."

Barrett did not know how to disagree with that statement without upsetting the beautiful blue-eyed woman who had her hands placed on each side of her hip with her head tilted. He knew she was daring him to comment further. He shook his head. "I know I cannot win right now. So, I'm gonna be the bigger bear and back off."

"Wise decision, sir. And since our conversation has gone this far, my name is Camryn Griffin. And yours is?" Camryn held her hand out, as if to make amends for their altercation.

Barrett was very rarely taken by surprise, but this gesture took him off guard. She shook her hand in the air as if to say, I'm only going to do this one time and one time only. He reached out his hand. Her hands were soft and warm. Her hands were petite in size. Very long, slender fingers. Her nails were covered in a light pink nail polish. It was not dramatic or scene-stealing. They were delicate. She took his hand with a small squeeze of strength. Camryn wanted him to realize she was not a "buttercup" female. She did not want to appear weak or helpless. Especially, in trying to maneuver the shuttle to the hotel.

Barrett could not help but admire her. Had he missed her checking in for her ticket? Were they on the same flight? He pondered what her business could be for the trip? He knew those handshakes. He had shaken too many hands at the conclusion of business deals to not know what a "handshake" meant.

Okay, two could play the game. He could see she was trying to be patient. Barrett had yet to reveal his name. He inhaled slowly, to make his voice huskier in response. "My name is Barrett Drew, and when I tell you, I mean it, it's truly my pleasure to meet you. You did say your name was Camryn?"

"Yes, it is. And yes, the name Camryn may be given to the male population, but it is truly my name. Since, we now know names, where are your travels taking you? Other than the hotel right now?" She smiled.

Barrett was taken aback by what her smile was doing. He wanted to please her with his answer. Why? Why should this young woman be impressed by him? Barrett replied, "I am just returning from a business meeting. A merger has been finalized for my company. I am returning back to meet our board and go over any last-minute details. And you?" He couldn't help but repeat her question. "Travels – where are your travels taking you?" This question had been posed to him millions of time, but not with these exact words or with the inflection she stated. She seemed to genuinely care why he was flying.

Before Barrett could mull over any other alternative to Camryn Griffin's question, the shuttle pulled up. The shuttle driver came to the curb where all the passengers from the flight were standing and stated that he would take couples first, to keep them together and then come back for any remaining singles.

As Barrett watched the "couples" board, he burst out laughing. Camryn also noticed this as well. She looked over at him. "You've got to be kidding me. We are the only singles on this flight!" Barrett nodded. "Don't worry, I'll wait with you. You won't be single. You'll have me."

Camryn shook her head. "Just so you know, moving forward, as we arrive at the hotel destination, I'm fine being single."

The shuttle doors closed. And the next shuttle moved into position. Barrett looked at her. If left up to Barrett, she would not be single for more than a night.

CHAPTER 5

Camryn had made the decision that she was not going to sit too close to him on the shuttle. Well, that decision was taken out of her hands. The remaining couple had positioned themselves. There were two seats left. Of course, they were side by side. No separation. He watched as she was surveying the shuttle. Barrett knew she would realize there were no more choices. Camryn had to sit beside him. He motioned for her to take the seat near the window.

"If okay with you, I'll take the outside seat," Camryn told him politely. She did not care which seat she needed to occupy, she needed to sit down. Camryn had to cross in front of him. She did not mean to, but it happened. Camryn could not avoid it. She was trying her best. Camryn brushed her breasts up against Barrett's chest. His eyes were watching her. She was under a spell. His spell. Her feet were frozen. He leaned close to Camryn. His whisper was almost too quiet for her to hear. But she did. Barrett's whisper was husky. "You won't be sitting too long," Barrett winked.

Camryn sat down. She was feeling lightheaded. Whether from not having food for a few hours or whether from his close proximity. Either way, she needed a bed to lie down.

Registration was a breeze. Camryn had to admit that more than likely, the airline must have had this type of problem before and knew how to handle delays and keep their passengers happy. Camryn picked up her briefcase that she had laid in front of her feet. She reached for her overnight bag. Turning to head to the elevators, she heard him say, "Wait, I'll ride up with you. I'll make sure you get safely tucked away."

"Oh, I can do my own tucking." Camryn grimaced. Where were these words coming from? She sounded like a teenager. As Camryn was pondering her next move, he was holding the elevator door for her entry. Several more had taken Barrett's kind gesture and were walking on. Okay, she thought, it's just not me on here with him. As the elevator doors opened to the floor numbers pushed, Camryn watched them leave. What were the odds that he and she would be the last individuals left on the elevator? Probably one in a million, and yet, here she was. All alone with him in close proximity and nowhere to go.

Before she could overthink this predicament, Barrett cleared his throat. "Well now. Only one button lit on the elevator panel. My investigative eye tells me we are on the same floor."

Camryn was ready to make a snide comment about how astute his "investigative eye" was when the elevator jumped. Camryn had always hated elevators. Elevators were too confined and too small. She dropped the briefcase and reached for the railings with both hands.

Camryn's fear of elevators was well-founded. She had been walking onto an elevator a few years ago, delivering a package to a friend's business. Without warning, the elevator doors began to shut on her. She could not escape the claws of death that forced her to drop the package on the inside of the elevator while trying to back out. There was no one on the inside to push the "door open" button. There were several around who had jumped in to try to pry the claws of death apart, but to no avail. She was in a horror movie. Her last thought was that her arm was going to be ripped off.

Camryn shook herself mentally back to the situation at hand. The elevator was stopped. It had not fallen. She was still standing upright. She began to hyperventilate. Could this day get any worse?

Camryn looked at him. She could tell he was genuinely concerned about her because he was walking towards her in that small, confined space to make it even less spacious.

Camryn put her hands out. "Don't. If you touch me, I'll probably scream, and it's not because I'm scared of you. It's because I have a fear of elevators and all my worst nightmares are coming true again."

Barrett could sense she was at her breaking point. He saw that wide-eyed deer-in-the-headlights look. He threw his hands in the air. "It's okay. I'm not going to come any closer to you. Watch me. I'm just going to push the emergency button, so the hotel administration realize we are stuck."

He did just as he said. He turned towards her. "I do not know how long it will be before someone comes across the intercom system, but I know we will not be stuck forever. Since we are going to have a few minutes, it appears, let's sit down and relax. Maybe we should get to know each other." He winked to try to reassure her.

"Winking at me does not reassure me. Getting me out of these close quarters would put you on my top five list of individuals I like. I'm not sure how much longer I can hold on to my dignity before I truly embarrass myself further," Camryn replied. Barrett could tell she was beginning to panic. He heard the desperation in her voice.

"We've both had long days. I must confess. I'm tired. I figure you are, as well." Barrett slid down the elevator walls. He patted the elevator floor with his hand. "It's definitely not the Waldorf, but it will do in a pinch. Right now, we are in a pinch. Plus, it will be our secret. I promise I will not tell any of the other passengers you actually agreed with me. Your reputation of being a 'kick-ass' woman will not be tarnished."

Camryn could not help but smile. "Well, since my secret is safe with you and you promised, okay." As Camryn positioned herself against the elevator wall, she reached for her briefcase. She needed to know that it was close to her body. Even though there was no chance that anyone would steal it. It was just her and Barrett. She saw his briefcase beside his leg. It was similar to hers.

Barrett was watching her emotions run across her face. An unfamiliar feeling of wanting to protect her slipped into his thoughts. Why? And why now? He knew he could not sit in silence, and the next step was obvious. He was sitting on the floor. What the hell, he thought. She can only remain quiet. So, he did the obvious.

CHAPTER 6

"Since we are stuck together, we might as well make the most of it. Tell me what's in your briefcase, and I'll tell you what's in mine."

Camryn laughed. She had to give him credit. Most would have probably sat in silence. Not him. And for that, she was grateful. She needed something to take her mind off the feeling of isolation.

Her smile was a bit shaky, but it was followed by, "Now, if I tell you my secret, then it will not be a secret. Where does that put me on your friends you can trust list and not?"

He couldn't help it. She had him. Once a secret was told, it was no longer a secret. One word spoken, and the cat was out of the bag, so to speak.

"Let me rephrase the question then. What brings you to Coastal Wind, Nevada. There, how's that? Not too intrusive, and your secret is still safe. More so, from the way you are holding tight to your briefcase, it is still locked away."

Camryn looked down. She had not realized how red her knuckles had become holding on to the handle of her briefcase. She looked at the briefcase and then at him. He was right. He would not reveal anything. He did not know her, and chances were he did not know her family background.

She tilted her head. "This could take a while. But as you have repeatedly stated in the last five minutes, neither one of us can go anywhere."

She took a deep breath. This was the first time she was telling the story. "I had family business to conduct. My parents were... I'm sorry, my parents, passed. I was meeting with an attorney to go over the administration of their estates. It was only about an hour meeting. When I left, I was handed this." She lifted the briefcase and placed it in front of her face. The briefcase made a thud as she placed it back on the floor of the elevator.

Barrett crinkled his eyebrows. She caught his confused look. Before she could begin adding how they passed, he interrupted with an apology. "I'm sorry you lost your parents. I'm sure there is a lot of paperwork that must be dealt with."

She held her hand up. Camryn never knew how to accept someone being so kind that did not even know who she was. She had no inclination to share what her career was. Some things were meant to be kept private. "Now, your story. What brings you to Coastal Wind, Nevada."

"My trip was just to merge two companies together. Nothing major. We had, just like you, paperwork to deal with. Both sides left the table happy with the outcome. I am now returning home and back to business as usual."

Camryn nodded. "It seems we both have a lot to review when we get back home."

Before she could inquire where home was for him, a voice from above could be heard. "We are correcting the situation of the stalled elevator. The doors will be opening shortly."

Camryn and Barrett looked at each other. They heard the noise of the elevator moving. In sync, they both began to pull themselves up into a standing position.

The elevator jostled. The movement caused Camryn to fall into Barrett. She could not steady herself with the elevator banister. There was no way Camryn could stop her full weight from falling into Barrett. She smashed into a strong chest. Without thinking, Barrett reached around her waist and pulled Camryn close, to brace her unsteadiness.

Camryn steadied herself. Barrett was still holding her tight to his chest. She pushed away, only to hear him say, "There's nowhere to go, except here. I got you."

There was no escape until that elevator door opened. Why was it taking so long? And he was still holding her.

The doors opened. He dropped his arms away. Camryn stepped back. She reached for her rolling luggage carrier and her briefcase. Barrett reached for his luggage and briefcase at the same time. His hand brushed hers. Camryn snapped her hand back. An unfamiliar burning sensation ran through Camryn.

He observed her nervousness. Was it from him? Was it from being trapped in the elevator too long? He was going to assume the latter. He could be charming, contrary to what the company employees thought.

Barrett motioned with his hand. "You first." Camryn laughed. "Going to make me test the waters, to see if the door closes on me."

Barrett shook his head. "Well, I was trying to showcase my manners, but evidently, I need to be chivalrous to capture your attention. He positioned himself in between the elevator doors. Barrett looked Camryn in the eyes. "Feel safer now?"

Camryn knew he was teasing her. She had no idea why she did what she did. But she did it without thinking about any repercussions it may cause. Camryn touched him on the sleeve to acknowledge his kindness.

As he stepped off behind her, she was looking to see which way she should be turning to get to her room number. Before she could take the first step in that direction, Barrett placed his hand on her elbow, to guide her towards the right. Again, another jolt of warmth shot through her.

He knew he had an effect on her. Her cheeks had turned a warm, pink hue. "Wouldn't it be funny if our rooms were beside each other or across from each other?"

Camryn turned quickly. "You're joking. Do you know something that I do not know?"

"Calm down, Camryn. I know nothing. Let's doublecheck to see what our room numbers are again." Barrett replied, "Mine is Room 601. What's yours?"

Camryn could not help but roll her eyes. "Room 603. Side by side. More than likely, there are connecting doors, too."

"You're so sure, aren't you? Did you plan this, Barrett? Camryn tilted her head, giving him that, "I don't believe you" look.

"Now, how on earth would I work this kind of magic in a hotel that I've never stayed at. Let's just call what it is."

"And, pray tell, Mr. Barrett Drew, what shall we call it?" Camryn laughed.

"Some would say kismet. Some would say coincidence. But I'm going to say destiny," Barrett winked at Camryn.

Camryn's eyebrows drew together. "I do not believe in kismet, coincidence, or even destiny. But I don't look to the future. I'm here in this moment. And as of this time, you are in my moment. When I wake up in the morning, my journey continues in a different direction than yours. If I'm not sure of anything else, I am sure of this."

Barrett nodded his head back and forth. "You are tired. You need to get some rest. I'm pretty sure I know what I am talking about." With no thought to the outcome, he placed his hand lightly on her back and gently nudged her in front of her door number. "Like I said, get some rest. Tomorrow is another journey with more moments."

She watched as he stood in front of his room and placed the door key inside. As he opened the door, Barrett looked back at Camryn. "See you bright and early in the morning for more adventures," and just like that, the door closed.

Camryn did not move. What just happened? Before she could think of any more questions, she inserted the door key. She opened the door. A big, king-size bed was all alone in the room. It was inviting her. She laid the briefcase she had been clutching down, along with her luggage. She inhaled. Did she want to look inside the briefcase or wait until she returned home? She looked at the briefcase. It was not going anywhere. It would be here in the morning. It could wait.

She changed into her pajamas. She lay down on the bed. Her last thoughts were, *He is less than five feet from me. I am safe.*

CHAPTER 7

He heard it. He heard it again. It was a scream. It was a scream of panic. Barrett jumped from the bed and stood to make sure he was a bit more alert. There it was again. It was coming from her room. He walked to the adjoining door to their rooms. He could hear the uncontrollable cry from her room. Barrett clinched his hand in a fist. Pounding with all his weight on the door, he hollered, "Camryn, are you okay? Answer me! Answer me, now!"

He had raised his hand to begin the barrage of pounding again. Before his fist could hit the door, he heard the lock turn. He stepped back.

She was sobbing. She looked at Barrett. "It was a dream. That's all it was. I'm fine. I promise." And then, she fainted. Barrett caught her. He scooped her up. He walked to the end of her bed. He sat down, with her body held tight to his. Barrett looked down at Camryn. Her breathing had slowed. She was coming back to him. He watched as her eyes slowly opened. Barrett knew Camryn was assessing where she was.

There was no explainable reason why she instinctively knew she was safe. She felt the heartbeat. She felt the warmth. The last thing she recalled as she closed her eyes to rest from the flight delay was the news that she had received that her parents had passed. The day was embedded in her mind. It was the worst day ever. In less than five seconds, her entire world had crumbled.

Taking her hand that was free, she wiped away her tears. She maneuvered herself so she could look at him. Camryn knew she had scared Barrett. His eyes revealed his concern.

He did not expect his reaction to her shifting within his arms. Barrett stood up before she could see. He made sure Camryn was standing upright. He was unsure if he should leave and return to his room or stay and comfort her. He was leaning towards the latter. But that decision was taken out of his hands by the knock on the door. "Miss Griffin, is everything okay? Are you okay?"

It was the front desk attendant. Camryn walked towards the door. She peered through the peephole, just as a precaution. She turned to tell Barrett thank you. The adjoining door to their rooms had already closed. He had left silently and without a word. She unlocked her hotel room door and opened it to the young woman standing outside. Her name was Eve. Camryn had remembered her kindness when all were checking in.

"I'm sorry, ma'am. We received a telephone at the front desk that there was screaming coming from this room. Again, are you okay, Miss Griffin?"

Camryn nodded. "It was just a bad dream. I'm fine. Really, I'm fine."

Camryn did not know if Eve believed her or not, but Eve placed her hand on Camryn's arm. "If you need anything, please just call the front desk. I have night duty."

Camryn nodded in agreement. "I will. I promise." Camryn watched as Eve walked the long hallway of rooms and then turned left to where the elevators were stationed. She closed the door and pressed her back against the cold metal. She doubted she could fall asleep. Camryn walked towards the bed. Sitting down at the end, she could sense his presence from where he had sat at that same spot on the bed holding her, assuring her she was safe. Camryn shook her head. Was she really?

Morning came too early. Shower, pack, and a quick bite to eat, and she would feel better. She had to feel better. She needed to return home and learn what was in the briefcase. A perusal of the room for any leftovers that may have been forgotten was the last item on the agenda. Opening the door, she viewed the hallway to the elevators. Empty. There was no one. Camryn had not heard any movement from any occupants outside the doors as she was moving around in the room. Not even him. Had he already left?

Elevators. Standing. Waiting. The numbers being highlighted. Barrett had no idea how long he had been standing there, but evidently, a few minutes. A crowd was gathering. From the baggage placed by their side, it was the passengers from the delayed flight. He smiled and nodded a good morning to all. He did not see her. The doors opened.

One last look before he walked on. He did not want to admit he was worried. Barrett saw her behind others. She had placed her luggage carrier and briefcase down. Camryn looked directly at him. The elevator doors closed.

As she walked down the hallway to the elevators, she was met with good mornings from stragglers just like herself. She could hear conversation coming from the area of the elevators. As she was walking out of her room, she stepped back and leaned into the adjoining door. She could not tell if he was still there. Silence.

Turning the corner, Camryn could see there was a crowd gathered. She did not mind waiting. Not everyone could fit on those tiny elevators. There would be another. Watching as the first set of doors closed, she looked up. Camryn saw him. He was pushed in the back corner. He looked uncomfortable. The elevator doors closed.

He did not know whether to be relieved or concerned about Camryn. As the elevator doors opened, everyone breathed a sigh of relief as the exited. They would be on their way to their destination. Barrett looked at his watch. He checked his cell phone one more time, to be sure that he had the flight number and takeoff time correct. There was still time to get a cup of coffee in the hotel café and possibly, a muffin to boot. He walked to the cashier and paid. Looking around, he saw others had had the same idea. There were not many seats left, but he spied a small nook that displayed the outside and the bright morning. Barrett was eager to get home. Work would be unbearable with the new merger.

Stepping off the elevator into the lobby, Camryn needed to purchase a bottled water to take with her. She may even splurge for a croissant or some type of breakfast sandwich. Walking towards the small hotel café, she laughed. Everyone else had the same idea as she did. She pulled her cell phone out of her purse. The flight was still going. Times were still confirmed. No changes. This was good. She would be back home before it got dark. If Camryn were honest with herself, she did not want to know what was in the briefcase. An ominous feeling had been lingering since she had touched the briefcase. Paying the cashier, Camryn looked around. There were no seats available. She sensed, rather than saw. Barrett stood up and motioned with his hand to join him. Of course, there was only one seat left in the entire café. Why not? What could happen? They both were boarding their flights to their destinations. They would never see each other again. Right?

CHAPTER 8

He saw her. He sensed when she arrived. She had no choice but to sit with him. Most of the tables were already taken, and if there was not an individual sitting at the table, you could tell someone had earmarked with their luggage that the table was taken. Barrett could tell she was trying to avoid sitting with him. Why? He had been a gentleman this entire stay. If it were about last night's episode, he had left early from the room. He did not want to seem as if he were waiting to interview her.

Camryn acknowledged him. Barrett smiled. He was glad she had nowhere else to sit. Seeing her put him at ease with his concern. As Camryn approached his table, the only table left, she continued to look around, as if a just-in-case kind of moment would occur and a table would appear magically available for her, and her alone. That was not the case.

Before she could become leery of his intentions, Barrett stood up and pulled the chair out for her. He deliberately sat across from her in the cushioned seats. "Thank you, Mr. Drew."

"Oh, so it's Mr. Drew. Last night, I could have sworn you used my first name. I'd rather stick with that today. Mr. Drew sounds so impersonal. Holding you in my arms last night was definitely not that."

Camryn placed her finger on her lips. "Ssssshhhh, someone may hear you. They may think that something went on between us. We've only known each other for less than twenty-four hours. I don't want them to think I used you as a one-night stand."

Barrett could not help but laugh so hard. "You used me as a one-night stand. I'm pretty sure, Camryn, they would not think that of you. Maybe me. But definitely not you. Let them come to their own conclusion then. Both you and I know that nothing happened. You were in need of comfort, and I was there. Eat your breakfast. And then, we will be on our way. Headed back to the airport to catch our flights. Your reputation will remain intact."

Camryn smiled and looked at Barrett. "I'm sorry. Just information overload. I know arriving home will put my mind at ease when I am able to view the contents of my briefcase. Thank you for being chivalrous last night. I do appreciate your kindness and your discretion."

Barrett knew she was genuine. The inflection of her statement resonated her true spirit. "I do understand the need to get home. Finalizing the merger I told you about is my highest priority."

Camryn dabbed her mouth with the napkin. She pulled out a small, round compact from her crossover bag. She placed lip gloss on the tip of her index finger and then slightly smoothed over her lips. Barrett was mesmerized. He followed the direction of her finger over her lips. Her lips became swollen and pouty. The only thought that came to his mind was Camryn needed to be kissed.

Camryn looked at him. He was staring at her. What now? Did she have something in her teeth? Camryn thought she had done a double-check on this matter. Barrett stood up and was pulling her chair out for her before she could inquire. "It's almost time to get back on the road. Our destination awaits us. I'll pay for it. My treat, okay?"

As Barrett watched as she absorbed what he had just said, the word "treat" was stuck in his mind. It would be a treat to spend a few more minutes with Camryn. He had not meant to place his hand so low on her back. He was just mere inches from heaven. Motioning her to his side, so he could pay, he noticed there was little room for her to stand because of the customers realizing time was passing.

As he paid, Camryn placed her hand on his arm and lightly squeezed it. "You did not have to pay. I do have money. Thank you though."

That squeeze just put a thought into his head, and without worrying about any repercussions, Barrett kissed her on the forehead. "You're welcome. Come on, or we will miss the airport shuttle."

Walking down the hotel hallway, Barrett could see through the revolving doors of the entrance, the airport shuttle had just arrived. Barrett knew there would be two shuttles to return the passengers back to the airport. He wanted to be on the shuttle with her.

Approaching the hotel's revolving doors, Barrett motioned for Camryn to go in first. As Barrett entered, the doors slapped him in his chest. The strap of Camryn's carry-on was caught. The look of panic of Camryn's face and the passengers already entering the airport shuttle, pushed Barrett into motion. "Camryn, look at me. Your carry-on's strap is caught. Move back a bit, and I will pull, to see if release can be made."

Camryn nodded through the revolving glass doors. As Barrett pulled the doors in a backwards motion, Camryn reached down to jiggle the strap free. She landed on the floor but was able to give Barrett a thumbs up from the floor that she was okay. He could not help but laugh. No one at the office would believe THIS story. He watched as she positioned herself again and then slowly pushed the door. He reached for the briefcase to place it to the side. He made sure she was released and standing upright. As he exited the revolving doors, he laid his briefcase and luggage in between them. The driver of the airport shuttle looked at Camryn. "Ma'am, you must get on board. I must get you to the airport in time. There is one seat left. Please ma'am."

Without thinking or hesitation, Camryn reached down and grabbed her briefcase, placed her carry-on over her shoulders and looked at Barrett.

Camryn looking at him was Barrett's undoing. An emotion he had not experienced was invading his senses. Loneliness. He did not want to leave Camryn. With all that was between them, the carry-on, the briefcase, her purse, Barrett pulled her close. His kiss was meant to be a goodbye kiss. That was not the case. She inhaled. Barrett could not let go. Camryn shut out the rest of the world, the death of her parents, the flight delay, the elevator entrapment, even the kiss at breakfast. The only thing on her mind was his lips and his breathing as the kiss became more intense. It was deep. It was dominating. Camryn had never been kissed like this before. Barrett's kiss was full of feeling and hope. The emotions arising from Camryn had never been there before. She did not want Barrett to stop kissing her. Camryn did not want to let him go. And yet, she did. She had to. She stepped back from Barrett's embrace and steadied herself. She approached the shuttle where the driver reached for her to balance her getting on the steps. The driver followed behind, positioned himself, and closed the doors.

Barrett watched as she walked through the shuttle crowd and finally sat down. He saw her peer over a few passengers. She was gone.

Camryn needed one more glance to be sure he was still standing there. Was Barrett Drew a dream? Was the kiss real?

CHAPTER 9

That corner. That corner was the dead giveaway that home was near. Camryn was tired. She had called her office to let them know what had transpired and that instead of working from home (as they typically did three days out of the week), she would return to work in the morning. At which point, Camryn would follow up on all concerns and contracts. Public relations and marketing with out-of-state clients had its advantages.

Being able to have the flexibility and work out of her home was crucial. Camryn had no objection to the nine-to-five job. It was the mere fact she did not want to "people." She had been with Cool, Creative, and Catchy Advertising Agency going on five years. Jesse, her assistant, had been with her three of the five years. He was her age. He was the one who could "people." Jesse never had a problem attending a meeting that Camryn did not want to. Camryn had confidence in Jesse, and so did the company.

Camryn remembered that Barrett was headed back to Conway CA. Two different flights. Two different states. Two very different lives.

A week had passed. It was still there. It was where she had laid it the night she walked in from the flight. Camryn had no desire or curiosity to unlock it just yet. As she walked through the kitchen and passed it again, she stopped. What was wrong with her? It was just a briefcase with paper inside.

Camryn wondered why the attorney had handed her such a masculine briefcase from her parents who had just passed away. It was silver. It was big and bulky. What did it hold inside?

She began fixing dinner. Getting the pan out to fry her salmon, she glanced back over her shoulder. It had not moved. She pulled some fresh salad from the refrigerator. Still there. One or two things were getting ready to happen. Camryn would make the decision to begin supper or her curiosity would grab hold, and she would starve until the briefcase was unlocked. Camryn walked to the living room and picked up her purse from the couch. She sat down at the table and began to search inside her purse. Panic set in. Camryn knew the key was there. She had placed it in a spot she would not forget. Evidently her memory could not be trusted. She dumped the entire contents of her purse on the table. She took her hands and waved over everything and began counting.

Camryn saw the one-dollar bills she had crumpled up and thrown in her purse after that morning's breakfast with him. There it was. Safely tucked away. She shuffled the dollar bills and pulled it out. How the tiniest of things could cause the largest of concerns. Sweeping the mess from the table back into her purse, she would organize everything later. Camryn pulled the briefcase closer. She took the key and inserted it into the first hole. Halfway in, the key stopped. She pulled the key back out and tried the second hole of the briefcase. There was a blockage. Something had to be blocking the entry. Why would the briefcase not take the insertion of the key?

There was no way this was happening. Camryn began to look at the briefcase. It was missing what she had feared. The marking was not there. Her initials, "CG," were nowhere to be found. Camryn had deliberately taken pink fingernail polish the night of the airline layover stay and had written her initials on the side. It was not large print, but it was recognizable to the naked eye. Camryn recalled making sure that she had double-checked the briefcase before leaving the hotel restaurant. The only time it had left her sight was when she got caught in the revolving doors and Barret helped her out by pulling the briefcase through and laying it to the side and then safely bringing her through the doors.

It was that kiss that had thrown her entire world off balance. Camryn looked at the briefcase. *Think*, she thought to herself. Two briefcases exactly alike. What were the possibilities? When did the switch take place? Better yet, how was she going to find *him*?

Time stops for no one. Within less than two hours from landing, Barrett had not had a moment nor the inclination to open the briefcase. He had even less time to think about scanning and reviewing the documents since arriving. Entering the office the next day, everyone was congratulating him on a job well done. He hated to admit it, but it was good to receive accolades when deserved. Barrett had been diligent with this merger, and it paid off. The Griffins had swung by his office this morning to do follow-up. It had been only a week since his return, but he knew they would want confirmation that all documents were received and handled accordingly. As they left his office, Barrett perused his calendar. He had a bit of down time. This would be the opportunity to open the briefcase and get his assistant, Chloe, to go through and scan. Since being employed there, the owners would always ask that he take this particular briefcase with him. He had no idea why. He never questioned it. The briefcase fit his personality. It was silver. It was big. It was bulky. It was roomy. He was pretty sure that there was not another in the world such as this briefcase. He had a feeling it had been handed down from someone who was very important to the Griffins.

He placed a call to Chloe to come in, so they could go through the contents together and get everything scanned and saved on the computer. He picked it up and placed it on the conference room table. Chloe walked in and smiled. "So, you were given the infamous briefcase to take on your trip?"

Barrett smiled. He liked Chloe. She had just graduated college with her associate's degree in marketing. Chloe was not afraid to offer suggestions to him. She was going to fit in fine at Vegas Heat.

Realizing as Chloe laid the briefcase on the conference room table, his instinct kicked in. This was not his briefcase. This one did not have scratches. His briefcase had scratches. What was worse, he noticed the "pink." There was no way in a million years that this had occurred. He had never lost this briefcase that had always been handed to him by the Griffins when he was doing transactions out of town. What's more, he knew.

Barrett looked at Chloe. "Chloe, please tell me if you see anything unusual about the briefcase." Why was Barrett asking her this question? She picked it up. It was heavy, just like always. It was bulky, just like always. And then she noticed it. It was a woman's initials. "CG" had been so lightly printed on the side. If she had not turned the briefcase over, Chloe would never have noticed. "I see it, Mr. Drew. I am not sure what it means, but I do see it."

"Thank you, Chloe. That's all."

Chloe had no idea what was taking place, but Mr. Drew looked frustrated. Turning to close the door, Chloe could not help but wonder if those initials had Mr. Drew more upset than the actual briefcase, itself.

As Chloe closed the door, Barrett knew he had the briefcase that belonged to Camryn Griffin. Trying to remember the incident, Drew could only surmise that after he did what he did – that kiss— that's when everything was switched. Barrett smiled. Camryn could not get on the airport shuttle quickly enough. He knew she felt it, too. They both had felt the entire stay at the airport hotel. Camryn must have handed his briefcase to the driver of the airport shuttle. Little did the driver know that two lives were changed within less than five seconds.

The next matter at hand was how to find her. He remembered the conversation in the elevator with Camryn. Her briefcase had held documents regarding the death of her parents. His merger documents were not important to him. He had already received the signed documents via email, and then they were scanned. Chloe had printed them and placed them in the client folder.

What was the name of the place where she worked? She had an unusual spelling with her first name, so this should not be a difficult search. He would begin the stalking phase of "finding Camryn Griffin" with Chloe's help. All things considered, the briefcase was not lost— it had only been misplaced.

CHAPTER 10

Camryn had called Jesse. He would know how to handle this fiasco. How did one flight become such a nightmare?

Sitting at the table with Jesse, Camryn couldn't help but laugh. They were so opposite, and that's what made them best friends. They complemented each other with their strengths. He had made a list of questions that he would need answered in order to find her misplaced briefcase. As he began the interrogation, Camryn stopped with him her hand in the air. "Wait, I remember. I remember where he works. It's called Vegas Heat."

"Such an easy fix," Jesse stated. He googled and pointed at the computer. "There it is. Vegas Heat. What a coincidence: it's in Conway, CA."

Camryn reviewed the website. She thought to the flight and then, it made sense. They were each in the middle of nowhere headed back to their somewhere. "I know I don't need to ask this, but are you going to call him, or are you going to make me call him?" Jesse inquired with an eyebrow raised. He already knew the answer.

"Please, can you call him? I am available on the weekend to fly and meet him and make the exchange. Please, Jesse." Camryn winked.

"Fine, but I am not flying with you. You are going solo. Just retrieve your briefcase, return his, and get back home. I want to know what's inside just as much as you," Jesse told her with a stern look.

Camryn knew he meant every word of it. As he dialed the telephone number of Vegas Heat, Jesse went ahead and placed the cell on speaker, so Camryn would be aware of the conversation.

"Vegas Heat, good morning," Camryn heard the receptionist's greeting.

Camryn was thankful for Jesse's words of professionalism. Before she could thank him, Jesse asked for the assistant of Mr. Barrett Drew. The receptionist said "Please hold a moment, and I will transfer you."

Jesse looked at Camryn. He chuckled. "Quit wringing your hands. He cannot see you through the cell phone."

"Mr. Drew's office. How can I help you?" Jesse relayed the story of being Camryn Griffin's assistant and that there had been a huge mistake with briefcases.

The next statement confirmed what Camryn had known. "Well, at least we don't need a search party established. We were looking to find you, and you have found us. Mr. Drew will be relieved. Hold on, and I will place him on the line with you." Camryn could tell the assistant was smiling on the other end of the phone.

He was watching Camryn through the exchange of his and Mr. Drew's assistant. He put his hand over the telephone speaker. "I'll be traveling with you. You might need my help."

Camryn was about to say something, when Jesse placed his hand over her lips. "No words of thanks are needed. It's a done deal."

This switch of briefcases could prove interesting, to say the least.

Camryn heard the call for boarding of the passengers remaining. Camryn pinched him on his arm. "Come on, sleeping beauty, they are ready for us."

Jesse opened his eyes. He looked at his boss. She was worried. It was a good thing he was on this journey with her.

Jesse and Camryn arrived at their airport destination, where memories flooded Camryn's mind. They checked in to their hotel. Jesse was two doors down from her. Camryn felt safe. Nothing could happen with Jesse being two doors away from her. Why was she nervous?

Barrett had given Camryn his cell, so she could text him upon arrival. Sitting at the desk in her hotel room, Camryn called his office. She wanted to let Barrett's assistant know they had arrived and were checked in. The office receptionist informed Camryn that Mr. Drew and his assistant had landed and would be at the meeting. Camryn stumbled a bit on her words. She had not expected Barrett to have "extra cargo" with him. Her first thought was they were probably sleeping together.

Camryn asked if the office receptionist could inform Mr. Drew's assistant, Chloe, and Mr. Drew that Camryn would meet him at the airport hotel café. "Absolutely, I will inform both. Thank you, and have a great day," the receptionist told Camryn.

It was the same café that she had eaten her last meal with Barrett. There definitely would not be any additional meals scheduled after this one.

Just the thought of being in his presence made Camryn shiver. *Concentrate*, she told herself. *He's not even standing in front of you, and your anxiety is taking over.*

Jesse knocked on her hotel room door. Camryn stepped back and told him to come on in. She informed Jesse of the conversation that had just taken place. Jesse watched her. *There she goes*, he thought to himself. *She's trying to map it out. She's trying to control the circumstances and how this meeting will play out.*

"Camryn, why don't you go ahead and take a shower and refresh yourself. Take your time. Gather your thoughts or whatever you need to gather in order to stand upright without passing out. I'll watch the news or channel surf. Once you are finished, I will return to my room and take my shower. Don't worry, it's just a briefcase exchange. What could go wrong?" Jesse tilted his head and winked.

CHAPTER 11

Barrett had given his assistant, Chloe, as many details as he could about the first accidental meeting between him and Camryn Griffin. Chloe nodded her head. "Barrett, I understand that this is only an exchange of briefcases, but something tells me there's more to the 'accidental meeting,'" Chloe relayed.

Arriving to the airport hotel, Barrett wondered what room had been assigned to Camryn. Checking in, Barrett requested the room where he and Camryn had stayed in the first time around. Approaching the hotel desk, Barrett pulled out his identification. "I've booked Room 601 for myself and 603 for my assistant. We are both checking in."

The hotel receptionist ran her finger down the computer screen. "Mr. Drew, I am so sorry, there was a mistake with the booking. We have you in Room 601, but Room 603 was already reserved for another customer. We have reserved 604 for your other party. I am sorry for any trouble this may have caused. This was entirely the hotel's fault. We will credit the room billing upon checkout. Everyone does have a room. Is this acceptable, Mr. Drew?"

Barrett had stopped listening when she had told him that Room 603 was already booked. Did she? Was the room booked by her? Without analyzing his words, Barrett immediately asked, "Who reserved Room 603? Is there a name you can give me?"

He caught himself and turned on the charm. He read her name badge. "I'm so sorry, Laney. I do realize you cannot give me this information…*but* can you at least tell me if it was a woman?"

Laney had encountered many good-looking men, especially in the hotel industry. He was quite the looker, and she could only imagine the charm he could exude. Laney shook her head no. "Mr. Drew, you know we cannot give this information out. It goes against our policies and procedures. But I do know she was very sweet."

She…Laney had said the pronoun "she." Okay, this was a positive. Now, how to learn who the "she" was.

Chloe could not help but laugh. "I don't want to even know why you wanted to know the identity of the individual in Room 603."

Standing in the elevator with her assistant, Jesse, and holding tight to the briefcase that belonged to him, Camryn recalled the conversation. They had agreed to meet at the airport café to exchange the briefcases. Nothing major. Nothing to be worried about. It was nothing out of the ordinary, right? Just two people exchanging a silver, bulky briefcase. Nothing could go wrong, correct? Two people and two briefcases. Would he recognize her? Stepping off the elevator, Jesse stopped her before they proceeded down the hotel hallway to the cafe. "It's going to be fine. It's just a briefcase."

He saw her turn into the hotel café. He also saw a man walking beside her. Chloe watched Barrett's face change from one of anticipation to one of caution. Chloe punched him in the side with her elbow. "Stop that. You don't even know who it is. It could be a family member."

"Stop what?"

"That look of disapproval. You know what you're doing. Stop trying to analyze and find the answer before you even ask the question."

Barrett was about to tell Chloe he was doing no such thing, when Camryn stopped. She looked directly at him. Barrett watched every step that Camryn took. Drawing her closer to him. Each step she took was purposeful. Barrett saw Camryn's eyes shift to Chloe. Barrett also saw the man with Camryn place his hand on Camryn's back. Why was Barrett feeling protective of Camryn right now? He had no idea who this man was, but he knew he was going to find out. There were no ifs, ands, or buts.

"Good morning, Mr. Drew. I hope you and your girlfriend had a pleasant trip."

Chloe was in the middle of drinking her cup of coffee. She almost choked hearing those words. "Oh, I can promise you I am not his girlfriend. Never have been. Never will be."

Barrett looked at Chloe. "Really, I'm that bad?"

Camryn liked her. Jesse couldn't help but laugh. He tried to hide it. Barrett looked at Camryn. "Well, I may inquire the same."

Camryn nodded. "Yes, you can."

Chloe smiled. Her boss had met his match. Chloe watched as Barrett tilted his head. "Well, Ms. Griffin, did you and your boyfriend have a pleasant trip?"

Jesse looked at Camryn. "May I set the record straight, since you two are fumbling over yourselves with jealousy."

Camryn rolled her eyes. "Why not?"

"I am Ms. Griffin's assistant and close friend. I have not, nor will I ever be her boyfriend. She is like a sister to me."

Chloe listened as Jesse stated his relationship with Camryn Griffin. Jesse must have read Chloe's thoughts. "Chloe, would you like to accompany me to another table, so the two lovebirds here can exchange whatever it is they are supposed to exchange?"

"Thank you. Yes, I would love to enjoy my breakfast

with you," Chloe winked.

As Chloe motioned for Barrett to move, Jesse told Camryn. "See, not so bad."

"I'll be over here if you need me. And, oh, Mr. Drew, Chloe will be just fine with me, as well. You two reminisce and let us know when the deed has been done."

Camryn chuckled. "Thank you. I owe you."

Jesse nodded in agreement. "Damn right you do."

Barrett watched as Camryn's eyes latched on to him. He could tell she was down to business. Before he could utter the next word, she dug in with "I think you have something that belongs to me."

Barrett looked Camryn up and down with such intensity. She did not know if he was going to hand over the briefcase, and then, he said, "Yes, I do have something that belongs to you."

Walking close to him, she held her hand out to receive her briefcase. Barrett placed it in her hand. "And now mine?" Barret stated as a question.

Camryn picked up the briefcase belonging to Barrett. She did not expect their hands to touch. Barrett's touch was intimate and personal. It was a slow placement over the top of her hand. He had not removed his hand.

Barrett watched for Camryn's reaction. He did not want to remove his hand. If he did, she would leave. Barrett wanted her to stay. Stepping back with his briefcase and placing it on the floor near his seat, Barrett stated the obvious. "It looks like my assistant and your assistant may need a few more minutes to finish their meeting."

Camryn nodded while trying not to laugh at his statement. "On this point, I will agree with you."

Camryn placed her briefcase by her legs and sat down. "Well, what should we talk about?"

Camryn thought it would be difficult to have a conversation with him. She was wrong. It was as if they had been friends for a while and were just catching up on each other's lives. Barrett had not enjoyed a woman's conversation as he did today.

Before they knew it, Chloe and Jesse were standing up. Jesse approached and stated, "Well, it looks like you guys have made up. Ready to go to our rooms, Camryn, and find out what's inside that briefcase?"

Chloe looked at her boss, too. "Barrett, are we good to go?"

Barrett and Camryn looked at each other. Yes, everyone could return to their rooms and their normal lives.

As the hotel elevator doors opened, Barrett motioned for Chloe and Camryn to walk on first. Barrett observed Camryn as she pushed the number for Floor 6. No one else made any comments about pushing any additional numbers.

Jesse busted out laughing. "There is no way. What are the odds that we are all on the sixth floor?"

CHAPTER 12

Camryn could not believe it. She turned to look at Barrett with such a scowl. "You didn't…"

Before she could even finish that sentence, Barrett placed his finger on her lips, "No, I did not. I already can imagine what you are thinking. To put your mind at ease, I did request the room I had when I first met you."

Barrett withdrew his fingers from her lips. He watched as she pursed them together. Camryn's lips were swollen from his touch. If only she would allow him a nibble. Barrett would not be greedy.

The elevator stopped and the doors opened to Floor #6. Jesse motioned for Chloe to walk before him and then offered Camryn the same.

Chloe turned to look back at Barrett. "I'm going to get some rest before the evening and dinner. Please let me know if there is anything else needed."

Barrett nodded. "I will see you later, Chloe. Thank you."

Jesse followed Chloe to her room to be sure she got in okay. What a coincidence. Just like Mr. Drew and Camryn.

This trip and these two individuals were going to be the talk of the water cooler when they both returned.

Camryn had not moved. She was curious where Chloe's room was. Camryn watched as Jesse entered Room 602 and then Chloe entered Room 604. Should Camryn be worried or not?

Barrett observed Camryn. "They will be just fine. Quit worrying. It's just like you and me. Side by side and more than likely, adjoining rooms."

Camryn smiled. "It's not the side by side that worries me— it's the adjoining part. But he's a grown man, and it's none of my business." Barrett commented, "You are correct. It's not any of your business."

Barrett had already walked into his room. Camryn was the only one remaining in the hotel hallway. Something was missing. There was an anticipation that Camryn didn't know how to describe. She felt empty. Placing the card to unlock her door, she walked in and stood looking around. It was true. She was truly alone.

Chloe heard the knock. She walked to her adjoining door. She opened it. "Hey, Chloe." Chloe could not help but grin. Jesse was so obvious. "Hey, yourself," Chloe stated.

Jesse smiled. He liked Chloe. He liked Chloe a lot. She was very easy to talk to. He felt like a high school boy asking a girl out for the very first time.

Chloe could tell Jesse was nervous. "Jesse, since you are halfway in my room, would you like to come the rest of the way? It's okay to step over the line."

Jesse looked at Chloe. "Yes."

Chloe held her hand out and remarked, "Enter at your own risk, sir."

And their adjoining door was shut.

Barrett looked at his watch. No wonder his stomach was growling. It had been morning since he had eaten anything. He had taken time to open the briefcase to be sure the originals were still inside. They were as he had left them. All placed in envelopes, marked according to the name of the document with the date of execution.

Barrett had decided to take a catnap. He was not tired. He was restless. The catnap did not work. He tossed and turned on the bed and then lay his arm over his eyes to make it dark. Still, his thoughts were of her. Why was she invading his nap? He reached for the cell to call Chloe to see if she would join him downstairs for dinner. Chloe answered with a yawn. "Yes, sir. Is everything okay?"

Barrett chuckled. "So professional, Chloe. I just wanted to know if you are ready for dinner? I am. Okay, I understand. Yes, that's fine. Don't worry." Well, now that Chloe would not be joining him, his thoughts went to her.

Barrett stood up. Should he? Should he just leave it alone? Should he just go by himself? No. The only thing that could happen was that she could turn him down. Barrett raised his hand. He knocked on their adjoining door.

Camryn did not mean to, but it happened. She had fallen asleep on the bed. She had set the alarm for only thirty minutes. Evidently, she needed the sleep. She never heard the alarm. She did hear something else. A knock. It was a knock on the adjoining door. Maybe she was dreaming. Camryn rubbed her eyes. She heard it again. There it was again—a knock. She got up and walked to the door. She unlocked the adjoining door, and there he stood.

"Hey, you. I just called Chloe to check on her for dinner. I wanted to inquire if she wanted to come with us, but she told me she was still tired and just wanted to eat room service. Would you be interested in attending dinner with me? My treat," Barrett stated with emphasis on the word treat.

Camryn could only concentrate on the word "treat."

Barrett could tell she had just woken up. Her eyes were still warm and hazy from sleep. Without any regard to the circumstances that might follow, he pushed a tendril of hair that had escaped behind her ear. With no thought for what she was doing, Camryn leaned her face into his hand.

Distance was not an issue. And then she asked. "Would you like to kiss me, Barrett?"

Barrett could not respond with a yes or no. He rubbed his thumb over her lips. Barrett pulled her closer to him. He placed his hand under Camryn's chin. Her lips were forbidden fruit. Just a taste was all that was needed. Leaning forward, he kissed Camryn. She returned his kiss. Her kisses were like that of a sweet wine. To hell with it. There was something between him and Camryn. It was so from their first encounter.

Barrett pulled his lips away. He watched for Camryn's reaction.

Camryn placed her fingers to her lips. "I guess I have my answer."

Barrett smiled. "Yes, you do. Are there any other questions that come to mind that need to be answered?"

Camryn looked at him. She felt safe. She felt warm. She felt emotions she had kept hidden. She could feel her cheeks reddening. Desire was the first word invading Camryn's thoughts. She desired Barrett. She was pretty sure he felt the same. She knew better than to ask that question.

"No. I think I've asked one question too many. The next may really get me into trouble," Camryn blushed.

"Then how about we go get dinner? Chloe has decided to stay in tonight, and if my guess is accurate, Jesse will be staying in tonight as well. There's no need to call him."

"What do you mean he's staying in for the night?" Camryn asked.

"Camryn, put two and two together. They have adjoining rooms, as you and I. I saw them before we came up on the elevators. I'm pretty confident the adjoining door has been unlocked and opened. Let's get you something to eat and then we will unlock your briefcase to see what secrets it holds."

Camryn did not want to argue with him. He was probably right. She had seen the exchange between Jesse and Chloe. She was hungry. Camryn had an ominous feeling with the briefcase. Call it intuition, Camryn knew unlocking that briefcase and those contents inside were going to change her life. Was she ready for it?

CHAPTER 13

Thinking there may be a wait for a table, both Camryn and Barrett were surprised they were seated upon walking into the hotel restaurant.

Their orders were taken. As the waitress repeated Barrett's order, Camryn noticed the waitress's eyes were lingering suggestively on Barrett. This was way too much for Camryn to accept without making a comment. Manners were way overrated in this moment. Camryn thanked the waitress for repeating their orders and said, "If we need anything else, I will let you know."

Barrett waited until the waitress had turned for the kitchen to deliver their orders. "Camryn, don't you think that was a bit stern? After all, she was only doing her job. Jealousy does not become you." Barrett knew he had hit a nerve. He watched as Camryn could not help herself.

"Jealous? I'm not jealous. She had already taken our orders. She had even repeated our orders to confirm there were no mistakes. There was no reason for her to procrastinate in turning our orders in or for that matter, to remain standing at our table and waiting for what? Your approval?"

Barrett laughed. He shook his head. "There's a saying in the play *Hamlet* by William Shakespeare that comes to mind, 'The lady doth protest too much, methinks.'"

Camryn knew he was right. She was just a "bit" jealous, but she did not want Barrett to know. "I just don't want to wait two hours for our food. I'm thinking of you and me."

"Whatever you want to call it, it's fine with me. I'm flattered you are concerned about me and care whether I am hungry or not," Barrett smiled.

Camryn knew he was teasing her. She enjoyed the banter back and forth. They began talking about their jobs. Camryn was curious about Vegas Heat and what Barrett's job title and responsibilities held.

Barrett knew she was changing the subject. That was fine with him. He would play along. He loved talking about his job. Barrett loved the owners of Vegas Heat, Lily and Everett Dean. At the water cooler, they were referred to as the dynamic duo. As long as Barrett had been employed at Vegas Heat, he had never heard mention of any children that the Deans may have had. It had always just been the two of them.

Without realizing she had commented out loud, Camryn replied to his last statement of "no children," "That must be sad. My Mom and Pop Pop spoiled me and supported me in my dreams, no matter how difficult they may appear or how silly."

Barrett watched as Camryn's face lit up when speaking about "Mom" and "Pop Pop." He could tell she loved her parents.

Camryn tried to mask her yawn. Camryn stood up and reached for their dinner ticket.

Barrett stood as well. He placed his hand on top of hers. Camryn remembered that touch. Before she could catch it, her cheeks began to blush. "No, Barrett, I'll pay this time. You paid last time, remember?"

Barrett did remember. That was also their first official kiss, if that's how you wanted to label a "first." And why should there not be more? Throwing caution to the wind, he entwined his hand through Camryn's. He pulled her towards him. "I do remember, Camryn. And I also remember the kiss. I think there needs to be a second kiss."

Camryn's lips betrayed her. She leaned into Barrett. His lips were just a whisper away. "Open for me, Camryn." He kissed Camryn's top lip and then the bottom lip. He heard the inhale of her breath. He did not want to let her go. There was more to taste of Camryn. He did not want just a few nibbles. He wanted more. Barrett realized he wanted her. "Let's go back to your room and finish this conversation."

Camryn could not find her voice after that kiss. She paid the clerk at the check-out. Thank goodness it was not the waitress who had served them their meal. Walking towards the elevator, Barrett kept his hand on Camryn's back.

Stepping off the elevator, Barrett guided her to her door. Opening the door, Camryn did not want to look back to see if had entered. She did not want to ask him to come in. What if she asked and he did not? Thank goodness he did not wait.

Barrett walked in. He could sense the tension in her back.

Camryn could not turn around. He would see how vulnerable she was. She hated that at times. She did not want him to see how much the kiss had affected her. If she turned, her emotions would be written all over her face for him to see. Barrett would know her need.

Camryn did not have to worry about turning around. She felt Barrett's muscular body against her back. He slid his hands through her arms to encircle her waist. Camryn was glued to the spot.

Barrett waited. Camryn had not moved. He could not see her face. One step and then two. Her back was to his chest. Camryn had placed her hair in a messy bun, which Barrett loved. His eyes were focused on pushing her jacket collar to the side. It gave him easier access to her neck.

"Camryn?" Barrett whispered. He heard her acknowledge him with an "hhhhmmm". Barrett's hand left Camryn's waist and began to remove the jacket. Camryn had a little white tank that hugged all her curves in just the right spots. Barrett's lips connected once more to Camryn's neck. Barrett reached up and pulled Camryn's hair down.

Barrett turned Camryn around. "Camryn, remember our first kiss was not planned. Our second kiss was. These kisses are meant for something more. Do you understand me?"

Camryn knew. He was asking her if he should return to his own room or stay. Camryn looked up at him. "I understand perfectly, Barrett."

Barrett pulled her close. He parted her lips with his finger. Camryn knew she never wanted him to stop kissing her. She raised up, so she could feel his lips. Barrett kissed her with such intensity. His kiss was deep. His kiss was full of something that Camryn had never experienced.

Barrett pulled back. He looked at Camryn. Her lips were swollen with desire. "Camryn, touch me."

Camryn did not know what he meant, until he brought her hand to him. Camryn felt Barrett's desire for her. She began massaging Barrett. She had never done anything like that in her wildest dreams. And yet, she wanted to.

Barrett slid his hands underneath Camryn's tank. "Let's

get this off of you." He began pulling her tank over her head. Pulling her closer, Barrett kissed the outline of Camryn's breasts. "And this, this is just in the way." He placed one hand on the back of her bra and with one turn, her bra had been unclasped. He reached for both the straps. Camryn watched as he pulled the straps down slowly, and then, there was nothing. She pulled her hands to her chest. "No, don't." Barrett placed her hands at her side. Camryn closed her eyes.

Barrett cupped one breast. He leaned down and kissed it. His thumb was magical. His thumb was circling the breast. He watched as Camryn's nipple became hard. As if this was not agony, his tongue mirrored the actions of Barrett's thumb. "Just a nibble. I'll take nothing more," Barrett spoke out loud.

Camryn inhaled. "Nothing more?"

Barrett smiled. "Do you want me to show you what more is, Camryn? There is so much more."

Camryn could not reply. She nodded. The strength of what was being built was beyond her comprehension.

"Stand still, Camryn. We have all night," Barrett told her.

Barrett rubbed around the sweet spot of the other breast. He did not want to leave any part of Camryn's body untouched from his tongue.

Camryn knew if he stopped, she would die. Emotions she had never known surfaced. It was as if someone else had invaded her body. Now was not the time to be shy. Camryn knew what she wanted.

Barrett did not know how much longer he could wait. He wanted Camryn to feel things that would take her to heights unimaginable when it came to making love. He unbuttoned her jeans. He thought about unclasping the pearl chain belt, but it was quite sexy on her nude waist. He took her shoes off and then shimmied her jeans down. "Step out, Camryn."

Camryn did as Barrett wanted. She was only left with her thong panties and that pearl chain belt on her skin. Barrett pulled her closer. He cupped the back of her bottom and followed the trail of the tiny thin line with his finger. Barrett did not want to take her thong off just yet.

Camryn stepped back. "Barrett, this is insane!"

Barrett could only chuckle. "No, Camryn, this is heaven."

He dipped his finger inside the panties. He followed her panties to the front of her belly button. His finger then moved inside of her. He separated her folds.

Camryn moaned. How much more could she take? Barrett knew he was close to that sweet spot.

Camryn shuttered against Barrett. Her legs were quaking. His finger was dangerous. Camryn felt Barrett slow down. "Camryn, there is no going back to just a kiss. I don't want just a kiss.

Camryn nodded. "I don't want just a kiss. I want you, Barrett Drew."

CHAPTER 14

That was all Barrett needed to hear. Barrett could not pull Camryn close enough to him. He needed to rid himself of his clothes. Skin to skin. That's what he desired.

Barrett stepped back and began pulling his shirt over his head. Camryn knew he was muscular. The man who stood before her took her breath away. She inhaled. Barrett kicked his shoes off and then his socks. The only article of clothing remaining between Camryn and Barrett were his pants.

What caused Camryn to step forward and reach for Barrett's hands, she had no idea. She had never been this brazen with any man before in her life. There was no time to evaluate the why. There was only Barrett.

Camryn began to unbutton Barrett's pants. The zipper slid down with such ease. Camryn knew Barrett's desire was there. She placed her hand on the outside of his jeans.

"Not yet, Camryn. Wait." Barrett pulled his pants down and stepped out of each leg. Oh, desire was not what Camryn was looking at. Barrett reached for Camryn. "Come here."

Barrett set about doing things to Camryn that he had

imagined since their first kiss. His fingers and his mouth were everywhere.

Barrett turned Camryn so that she could remove the chain belt. Unhooking the belt, Barrett pulled Camryn back. She felt it. She felt him. "Relax, Camryn. I only want to possess you body and soul. I will not ask for anything more than this."

"Turn around Camryn. Look at me. I make this promise to you." Camryn could only nod. She knew what Barrett was asking.

Barrett slowly placed his fingertip slipping between Camryn's wetness. He gathered her just to the brink of ecstasy. Barrett watched as Camryn's body responded to him. Time and space were non-existent. It was her.

Barrett led Camryn to the bed. He lay her gently on the bed. Barrett watched as she scooted to the middle. He slid into bed. She was petite. Barrett placed his hand on Camryn's waist and turned her. Camryn's back would be against Barrett's stomach.

Camryn did not know what to expect. Barrett could tell how Camryn's body was reacting. This was something new for her. Barrett began kissing her neck and then her shoulders, all the while pulling Camryn closer to his manhood. He felt Camryn shiver.

With one motion, Barrett positioned Camryn on top of his chest. Camryn could not resist. She began moving her body up and down Barrett's chest. "Camryn, I thought…"

Camryn smiled. "Yes, a lot of people do a lot of thinking about circumstances and situations. This is not one of those times. I want you, now."

Barrett laughed. Yes, a lot of pondering was taking place in Barrett's mind. They were thoughts of all the ways he could pleasure Camryn. "Then let me show you my 'thinking.'" Barrett positioned Camryn so that she was able to receive him. Slow at first, and then, he felt her acceptance of him. A rhythm had begun.

Barrett massaged Camryn's areola between his fingers. Her nipples were taut with need. Camryn knew it was building. An all-consuming desire to feel Barrett completely inside of her. Without warning to Barrett, she began the motion. He rubbed his forefinger across her lips. She opened her mouth and suckled on it. This was enough. Barrett could handle no more teasing.

With each thrust, Camryn and Barrett were as one. Camryn's legs grew tighter around Barrett's waist. Her legs quivered to indicate her fulfillment. Barrett placed his hands on Camryn's waist. She knew what he needed. "Tell me when to stop, Barrett."

"Never, Camryn, never stop." Barrett took a thrust that sent both Camryn and Barrett holding tight to each other. She knew when he had reached satisfaction. He sat up. She was still inside. Barrett was holding her and kissing her. Camryn returned the kiss with all her existence. Did Barrett know how he consumed Camryn like a fire?

Barrett slid her off him. He pulled her close to him. "Let's rest and then see what happens later."

What else could happen? This was perfection. Later. There would be a later?

CHAPTER 15

Barrett knew before he even opened his eyes, she was not there. He heard the shower. He would allow her privacy. Barrett waited until he heard the water turn off. He sat up in the bed naked, waiting for Camryn.

Camryn had closed her eyes. The warm water running had her imagination playing with her emotions. How could she face him? How could she open the bathroom door? She heard the movement of the bed. She knew he was awake. Pull the band-aid off quickly was the old saying. Wrapped in a towel, she opened the bathroom door. Camryn expected him to still be in bed, sitting up and definitely not naked.

Barrett stood. "Good morning, Camryn. Took you long enough. "I'll shower, and then, we can unlock the briefcase and then grab some breakfast." He kissed Camryn soundly on her lips. Barrett walked past her and shut the bathroom door.

Camryn blushed. It was not a question. It was a matter-of-fact statement. She was hungry, and she imagined he was as well.

Camryn had dressed. As the bathroom door opened, Barrett stood only in his jeans and tennis shoes. There was no shirt. Camryn felt something contract in her body. Was he going to cause this reaction every time she was near him?

He walked over to the table where the briefcase lay. Barrett kissed Camryn. "Now, your mind is on the kiss and not on that briefcase."

Barrett reached for the key that was to the side of the briefcase. "It's just one turn, Camryn."

Barrett placed the key in her hand. Camryn turned the lock. The briefcase was open.

There were so many pieces of paper inside. Camryn picked one up and began to read. Barrett was watching her reaction. The first tear trickled down her cheek.

Camryn looked at Barrett. "This is not real. This is a lie. It is made up. There is no truth to it. My entire life is a farce."

Barrett wiped her tears away. "What's a lie? What has happened, Camryn? What do the documents state?"

Camryn shoved the papers at Barrett. "Read them. They are not my parents. They are my grandparents. Read it, Barrett. I've been lied to all my life. They kept this secret their entire lives. They kept my identity from me."

Barrett began to read the documents. He started with the letter from the estate administration attorney. As Barrett turned the page over, his eyes caught the sentence that Lily Griffin and Reece Griffin were Camryn's true grandparents. Mr. and Mrs. Griffin had adopted Camryn after their one and only daughter, Lily Camryn Griffin had become pregnant by her high school sweetheart, Everett Dean. Mr. and Mrs. Griffin knew that their only child/daughter, Lily, wanted to attend college. Mr. and Mrs. Griffin knew Lily could not raise a child on her own and pursue her dreams of a business degree.

As Barrett got to that part, he stopped. He dropped the letter. He turned and sat down on the edge of the bed.

Camryn had no earthly idea was going on with Barrett, only the fact his eyes were as wide as saucers.

"Camryn, do you remember last night when I told you my employers' names?"

Camryn nodded. "I recall Davis or Dean, or a 'd' word."

Barrett replied, "You did not read the letter all the way through."

He handed her the paper. "This letter was written by the estate administration attorney on behalf of your parents, Lilly Griffin and Reece Griffin. There's more, Camryn. You stopped too early. Please read further."

Camryn was becoming frustrated by his insistence that she read it again. "I did read it, Barrett."

Barrett turned her face towards him. "Read it all the way through. One more time for me, please. Don't stop at the point where you saw the word 'adopted.'"

"Fine. Good lord. Barrett. I didn't miss anything. I read it. To make you happy, though, I will read it again." Camryn began to read the letter again.

She got to the part of where the Griffins had one child, Lily Camryn Griffin. Camryn dropped the letter to the floor. She looked at Barrett.

"It cannot be, Barrett. It just cannot be." Camryn stood up. Barrett knew. He caught her as she passed out.

Barrett smiled as he was holding Camryn. It was a good thing he recognized that she was going to fall into his arms.

He scooped her up and placed her on their bed. The next issue was to slowly wake her up. Barrett went to the bathroom and ran a washrag under the bathroom sink.

Barrett sat down on the side of the bed. He placed the cold rag on the side of Camryn's face. He had never had a woman to faint in his presence. Barrett watched as her eyes began to open slowly.

Barrett knew she was still a bit disoriented. "I'm here, Camryn. It's going to be okay. How about we read the documents again, and let's do it together. Can you stand up and make it back to the table again?"

Camryn knew she had scared him. When her eyes opened, there he was. She could see the concern, and she could sense the gentleness with which he was wiping her face.

"I can, Barrett. I'm okay." She sat up. She twisted, so she could touch him. There had been no time to speak about last night. She wondered if he was feeling the same as she was. Scared, terrified, afraid of all the emotions playing havoc with her. Barrett looking at her made the emotions more alert.

He reached for her hand and squeezed it. He smiled. Barrett pulled Camryn towards his chest. "I am not leaving, Camryn. One more look."

It was so nice to take direction from him. Camryn did not know what to do next. The rug had been pulled out from under her. She felt as if she had fallen straight on her back.

Barrett pulled out his ink pen and notepad. "Notes in a situation like this are necessary. I don't want to overlook anything."

Camryn couldn't help but laugh. What were the odds? "You think?"

Barrett leaned into Camryn. He kissed her on the forehead. "Yes, I think so."

CHAPTER 16

Barrett and Camryn had no idea how long they had been at the table reviewing the documents. The giggling in the hallway made them both look up from their concentration on the secret that briefcase held.

They heard the voices. Not one voice, but two. It was Chloe and Jesse.

Camryn and Barrett looked at each other. "You go open the door," Camryn told Barrett.

"Why me?" Barrett exclaimed.

"Why does the woman have to do it all?" Camryn tiptoed to the door to open it.

Barrett chuckled. "Why are you tiptoeing, Camryn?"

"Why else would I tiptoe on the carpet in our room with the door closed? I don't want them to hear me." Barrett could not argue with Camryn. If only she could hear herself and the explanation given. It made perfect sense to her. He watched her as she leaned out the door. It made perfect sense to him, as well. Barrett was in love with Camryn Griffin.

Opening a hotel room door that was heavy to begin with was a trick. She peered outside. There they both were. Chloe and Jesse. Jesse was in Chloe's doorway, trying to steal away one more kiss. Camryn watched as Jesse kissed Chloe one more time and then he was gone from the hotel hallway.

They were looking chummy. Camryn turned and whispered to Barrett, "Barrett, get over here."

Barrett figured what he had seen the day before had spilled over into the morning.

"Camryn close that door. Give them some privacy. They will tell us when they want us to know. It could be just a mutual evening of hot passionate rolling around naked in the bed lovemaking that stops when we board the plane, or it could be serious. Right now, it's none of our business."

Camryn hated to agree with him. It was not any of her or Barrett's business.

Sitting down, Camryn looked to Barrett. "What now? What do I do now? You know my birth parents. What happens Barrett? What do I do with this secret? Or the truth, as it has been revealed to both you and me?"

Barrett knew there was only one answer. Would Camryn do it? Would she take the step that would change not only her life but his life forever?

Chloe and Jesse had already arrived in hotel lobby. Jesse was standing in front of Chloe. He kissed her on the tip of her nose. "Thank you. Thank you for not shutting the door on me."

Chloe kissed Jesse back. "There was no way I could shut the door. You were standing halfway in my room and halfway in the hallway."

"I wonder what is taking them so long. Barrett told me to meet him in the lobby at 10:00 a.m. It's now 10:30 a.m. He is never late," Chloe commented.

Jesse laughed at the comment. "Well, when someone is thirty minutes late, there are two viable excuses. One is being sick and the other is something or someone else distracted your time. I'm going to say there was a big distraction."

Chloe and Jesse saw the elevator doors open and both Barrett and Camryn walked off together. As they approached Chloe and Jesse, Jesse could not help but remark, "I cannot believe you slept in, Miss Griffin. Was there something else or someone else on your mind? Maybe job related?"

Camryn knew he was teasing. "Jesse, if you only knew the half of it. It was not the 'someone' you are thinking about, but a secret that had been kept safely locked away for my entire life."

Jesse walked towards Camryn. "Do I need to do anything?"

Camryn shook her head no. "I'm not the person you thought I was. My name is real. But my parents are, in fact, my grandparents. And to top it off, Barrett works for my birth parents. The letter that was left by my grandparents revealed the truth."

Chloe sensed there was more ingredients to the story. She watched Barrett as Camryn told the story. Chloe watched as Barrett's hand slid to Camryn's back. Barrett's hand was placed with meaning. Chloe knew Jesse had yet to see what she was. Something had happened. Something was taking place right before her and Jesse's eyes with Barrett and Camryn.

Barrett looked at Chloe. Barrett knew his assistant. She had a keen eye for things that were out of the norm. Barrett could only imagine what conclusions Chloe was trying to narrow down. "Chloe, let's get checked out. I'll explain on the flight. We have a lot to do upon our return. The most critical right now is that Camryn will be coming to Vegas Heat next week. And from the looks of Jesse's eyebrows, Jesse will be joining her. Am I correct, Jesse?"

Jesse nodded. "Evidently, there is a who, why, what to this trip. She is not going to go into this by herself. Yes, I will be travelling with her to Vegas Heat."

"There was no doubt in my mind, Jesse. When Chloe and I return, we will make the flight and hotel arrangements for each of you," Barrett told him.

"Jesse, thank you for agreeing to accompany me. I know that I'm not just the only reason that you are travelling with me to Vegas Heat. When we arrive, we will need to schedule a meeting with Barrett and the owners." A tear formed. Camryn sniffed. She was not going to cry about this. She wanted to be mad. She could not. Her grandparents were her everything. They had done what was necessary in their eyes for her care.

"So next week, we leave. We leave to find out who Barrett's bosses are, which, in turn, are your birth parents. Did I state that correctly?" Jesse inquired.

"You did. I want to meet them. Barrett has agreed to tell them that we are new clients and will schedule a meeting for the first consultation of representation," Camryn calmly remarked. "I don't want to reveal that I am their daughter. They do not even know that my grandparents have passed."

CHAPTER 17

It was today. Today was *the* day. The flight, the arrival, the meeting. Camryn had been in contact with Barrett every day since returning home. She had made him promise not to tell anyone, and she had asked Chloe to please keep her secret. Both had agreed.

Jesse looked over at Camryn while she was driving. This news had turned Camryn inside out. Answers of her life had been locked away in that briefcase. Jesse could only imagine the lengths that Camryn's grandparents had gone to keeping Camryn's true identity a secret.

They pulled into the airport parking lot. Unloading, Jesse grabbed her and hugged her. He had known Camryn for a long time. He could see the tension in her body and the inhale of her breath. "You got this. Remember that one day you could not imagine having a child at Mom and Pop Pop's age, well, now you know. There was more involved to your birth than you ever dreamed."

Camryn returned Jesse's hug. He was not just a good friend, but a dear friend.

The plane landed. Camryn and Jesse had been given strict instructions that Barrett would arrive to pick them up and get them checked in to the hotel. There would be no need for a rental. He did share that Chloe would accompany him. Barrett had emphasized he would take care of anything.

Walking through the tunnel, Camryn stopped – "What if they don't' like me?"

Jesse was walking beside her. He knew she did not realize she had spoken her fear out loud. "Camryn, they will like you. You are their daughter. Quit overanalyzing the situation. Plus, if I know Barrett, he arrived early and is waiting impatiently to see you," Jesse stated with a wink.

Barrett could see the plane land from the window. He had not taken his eyes off the plane. He could see when the extender was attached so the plane's occupants could begin to exit.

He began to walk towards the flight check-in scanners. "Sir, can I see your pass?" Barrett was stopped dead in his tracks.

"All passengers will be coming through this way, sir, and you can wait over there," the flight attendant pointed out.

"There's only one passenger I need to see," Barrett told the flight attendant.

"I understand, but you cannot see her until she crosses through," the flight attendant was doing her best to soothe Barrett. Chloe was listening the entire time.

Barrett realized at that precise moment Camryn had his heart. There was no denying it. He was in love with his boss's daughter. He was in love with Camryn Lily Griffin.

Chloe grabbed his elbow. "You are going to get us thrown out of the airport if you don't behave and listen. I see them."

Barrett laughed. Chloe knew there was an attraction between him and Camryn. Chloe had walked in too many times into Barrett's office while he was on the phone with Camryn.

Camryn stopped. He was there, as he had promised. Chloe was standing beside him, waving and smiling as if she were waiting for long-lost family. Camryn doubted that smile was for her. From the corner of her eye, she could see Jesse smiling and throwing his hand up in acknowledgement.

Approaching the line of individuals going in the same direction as she was, Camryn could not help but notice that Barrett was standing in the way of everyone walking. What was he doing? He was not moving. He looked like a statute. As she got closer, Barrett walked towards her. Camryn did not have time to put her bags down.

Barrett could not stand it. He placed his hands around her waist and pulled Camryn close to his chest. "Hello, Camryn Lily Griffin." Before she could reply, Barrett leaned in. She knew it was going to happen. She needed it. She needed him to kiss her. Barrett pulled her tight to his chest. Luggage and all. There was nothing more he desired than to kiss her. In this moment, the world stopped. It was just his lips meeting hers.

Barrett's lips withdrew from Camryn's. She looked up at Barrett. He smiled. "Well, now that we have the welcome out of the way, let's get you and loverboy over there checked into the hotel."

Camryn laid her head against Barrett's chest. She laughed and said, "So, you noticed it, too?"

"How could you not?" Barrett stated as a matter of fact. "He was looking for her as much as I was looking for you."

Camryn caught those words. Barrett was looking for her. She was still holding on to the briefcase and her travel bag. "I'll take those, Camryn."

Camryn nodded her head no. "It's okay, I can carry them."

Barrett grinned. "Yes, I know you can carry them. I can, too. I'll take the travel bag. I know you want to hold on to the briefcase for security, but all secrets have been unlocked."

Camryn shook her head. "Yes, yes, you're right. It's just that it has been with me through this entire ordeal." Barrett understood.

Walking to the garage to Barrett's car, small talk was made. Nothing of importance. Both Barrett and Camryn commented on the reaction of Chloe upon seeing Jesse with Camryn.

"I'm going to take a bet that you are going to lose your assistant, Camryn. I have a feeling he may be left behind." Barret winked.

Camryn couldn't help but agree. She was sure of it. Camryn watched as Chloe placed her head on Jesse's shoulder. Would Camryn ever find that? A sense that she belonged.

CHAPTER 18

Barrett watched Camryn as she placed the card on the door for entry into her room for the weekend. He knew that Chloe had walked Jesse to his room, which unfortunately, was three doors away from Camryn, but then again, fortunate for Jesse. No one would be able to see if Chloe paid Jesse a visit.

Barrett knew she was tired and was also very confused about what was to take place in the next twenty-four hours. Barrett placed her on the bed. "Wait right here, please. I want to give Chloe Uber money, so she can leave without me, should she and Jesse want to eat out somewhere other than the hotel restaurant. I'll be right back."

Camryn nodded. "I don't plan on going anywhere. You're stuck with me."

Barrett thought to himself, if only he were stuck with Camryn.

Barrett returned and knocked on their hotel door. Camryn stood in the doorway. "May I help you?" Camryn smiled.

Whether she was teasing him or not, Barrett was thinking of all the ways she could help him. The first way was easing the pain of not touching Camryn.

"I'll keep that thought for later and take you up on it. But right now, let's get something to eat and discuss tomorrow."

The meal was great. The wine was sweet. The company was the best. Camryn enjoyed getting to know about Barrett before he came to Vegas Heat. Barrett was entranced as Camryn told him of her upbringing and her parents. Even though they were a bit mature in age to have Camryn, she never wanted for anything.

Realizing that tomorrow she would meet her birth parents, Camryn wondered what they looked like. Did she resemble her mother or her father?

Deep in her own worries, Camryn did not realize that Barrett had stood up. She did not expect Barrett's lips to be so close to her ear. "Are you ready for bed, Camryn?"

Walking to the elevator, Camryn stole a glance to look at Barrett. He had both his hands placed on the bars looking at her. "I promise you everything is going to be okay. You trust me, right?"

"I guess," Camryn stated. I have no reason not to trust you, correct?

"Camryn Griffin, why are you always answering a question with a question?" Barrett laughed.

"I didn't know I did. That's how my Mom would answer Pop Pop. Always with an answer in a question. It kept him on his toes."

Arriving at her hotel door, Camryn stopped. Camryn turned into Barrett's chest. If she were trying to get him to turn around and leave, this was not the way to do it. Barrett reached for Camryn's chin. "I don't have to leave Camryn. I can stay. Is that what you want?"

Camryn did not know how she did it, but she did. "Yes, please stay."

Barrett kissed her with a butterfly kiss. It was not sensual. It was not emotional. It was a kiss that was meant to offer comfort.

There was no thought of Chloe or Jesse. Barrett did not care. His only concern was the woman standing in front of him. "Do we want to see what's on tonight? We can watch a movie and just relax."

If only she could. She did want to relax. Whether that would occur was anyone's guess. She did not want to think about tomorrow. Camryn's only thoughts were that she had been bold enough to ask him to stay. Her life was changing right before her eyes.

Walking into the bathroom to change, Camryn emerged in her tank top and short sweats. With no regard to how it appeared, she climbed across Barrett to get comfortable on the bed. There was thought to consequences that they should be in separate beds.

Barrett wondered if she knew the effect she was having him by such a simple act. He doubted she knew how enticing that action of rolling across him was like striking a match. There was a fire that was raging inside of him for Camryn, and there was only one way to put it out.

Camryn was sitting against the back of bed just as he was. As the movie played, he noticed she was drifting off. Her head was laying against his arm. If he moved, Barrett knew he would wake her. It was better to let her sleep. The trip. This new information. The meeting at Vegas Heat. It would all still be here tomorrow.

Camryn felt the warmth. She did not remember turning the heat on when she laid down to watch the movie with Barrett. It was just enough she did not want to open her eyes. Her entire life had been a lie. She wanted to know why. She knew why the secret had been hidden from her. What of her birth parents? What role did they have in this?

Camryn opened one eye and peered at the clock. It was time. She sat up and placed her feet on the floor. Before she could realize what was happening, a hand came up and began to rub her back. "It will be okay, Camryn. One thing at a time."

Camryn jumped up and turned around. "Barrett, where did you … did we … how long …?"

"So many questions, Miss Griffin, and I'm not even dressed to answer the inquisition. Let me put your mind at ease."

"I did sleep with you. Did we make love? No. All night, I held you. You go ahead and shower first, and then, I will freshen up after you are done. I do not want you to be late, and I know you are worried about a lot. Go on."

Camryn could not fathom why she did what she did. Leaning in, she kissed Barrett on the lips. "Thank you for understanding."

It was so unexpected, Barrett was caught off guard. Barrett rubbed his thumb across her bottom lip. "I will tell you this, Camryn, one more kiss and we will be late to the meeting."

Camryn blushed. "I promise, no more."

Barrett laughed. "Oh, I will guarantee you there will be more, but not right now."

Camryn grabbed her clothes and toiletries and walked into the bathroom. She knew he was watching. She liked that he was watching her. Camryn closed the door. The saying that her Pop Pop repeated to her as a child when she was disappointed came to mind, "When one door closes, another door always opens. Just remember to grab the doorknob and push. It won't open by itself." Camryn would be ready.

CHAPTER 19

The morning was beautiful. The sun was not shining, it was sparkling. Camryn had called Jesse while Barrett was driving, confirming that Jesse would meet her there.

Jesse stated she was about fifteen minutes too late with the confirmation. He was already there with Chloe. Chloe was giving him the grand tour.

Camryn felt better. Jesse was a comfort. Someone familiar in her life. *It will be okay*, she tried to convince herself. Camryn realized there was nothing she could change. Mom and Pop Pop would never return. She did have another set of parents. Her birth parents.

Parking the car, Barrett saw her furrowed brows. There was no way in hell anyone could make this story up. Every detail bringing Camryn to this point was unbelievable. Not just for her, but for him, as well. Barrett reached for her hand. "Look at me. No matter what, no matter what is revealed, I will be right beside you."

Camryn squeezed his hand. "I don't know why, but I believe you."

Barrett knew. Barrett knew the why.

Stepping off the elevators, Camryn took a deep breath and peered out the doors of the elevator. "Where to now?"

"Breathe, Camryn. Your mom and dad have not arrived yet. They usually do not come in until around 9:30 a.m. That gives the staff time to gather documentation, agendas, questions for the week's preparation of Vegas Heat."

She stopped in her tracks. Barrett stopped too. He knew she had heard the reference, "your mom and dad." Camryn turned. "It's fine. They are my mom and dad."

Coming down the hallway were Jesse and Chloe. Camryn noticed Jesse's hand on the back of Chloe's waist. "Good morning, you two," Jesse began. "Everyone sleep well?"

Camryn could not help but smile. "Yes, and it looks like you two did, as well?"

Jesse turned towards Chloe. "See, I told you. Nothing to worry about."

Chloe shook her head. "I love you, Jesse Day." Jesse gave Chloe a quick kiss. "Well, you already know how I feel, Miss Chloe, vice versa."

Chloe looked at Barrett. "Now the hard part. Is the conference room suitable for the meeting?"

Barrett and Camryn looked at each other. They both heard the words. Barrett chuckled. "After that declaration, the conference room is ready."

Barrett and Chloe had left Camryn and Jesse in the conference room. Barrett needed Chloe to help tie up some loose ends with emails and telephone calls, but they would return with the owners of Vegas Heat. Camryn told them she and Jesse would be fine. Camryn reached for the briefcase. She opened it. They were only pieces of paper, correct? They were papers that have been locked away safely. It was a secret that had been kept hidden for over 25 years. What could go wrong?

Barrett opened the conference room door. He saw Camryn stand. Camryn smiled at him. He already knew. Barrett cleared his throat.

"Lily and Everett, why don't you guys take a seat here," Barrett pointed to the seats directly across from Camryn and Jesse.

Lily questioned Barrett. "Barrett, what is going on? Everett and I did not have a meeting scheduled this morning with any clients?"

"No, you didn't but I think you may want to meet this young lady. May I introduce you to Camryn Lily Griffin."

Barrett was watching Camryn. She had not moved. Barrett saw Jesse reach for her hand.

Barrett watched as he knew Lily and Everett were trying to make sense of this introduction and this unscheduled meeting.

Everett looked at his wife. "Lily, she is you. She is your twin." Everett turned his attention to Camryn. "Please tell us about you, Camryn."

Camryn could not believe it. Her birth parents were in the same room as she was. Camryn took a seat. She knew that if she stood, her legs would buckle. Camryn folded her hands on the table and began the story of her life she had only known.

"My parents just recently passed away. I received a telephone call from an estate administration attorney. I met him and he handed me a briefcase and told me to review the documents inside for what my parents had left me. After my briefcase and Barrett's briefcase were accidentally switched, I met with him to exchange. I opened the briefcase. Imagine my surprise, when I turned the key and inside the briefcase was not just documents but a secret. The secret that had been kept locked away. I am your daughter, Camryn Lily Griffin."

Camryn inhaled and looked at Barrett. "Barrett put two and two together before I did. And as the old saying goes, 'the rest is history.'"

Wiping the tears from her eyes, Lily stood. "Camryn, I want to tell you a story. It's not just a story of love, but it is a story of sacrifice. A decision made not in haste, but made for a life. Your life."

Camryn nodded.

"Your father and I were best friends for as long as I can remember. We were classmates in each other's homeroom from junior high to high school. We were inseparable. We knew what the other was thinking before it was spoken into the universe.

When I became pregnant with you, my parents/your parents, Lily and Reece Griffin, asked if they could raise you. They knew that Everett and I were too young, and they did not want to lose the connection with their first grandchild. Everett and I discussed at great length the life that would be altered and changed forever by this decision. Your parents made a promise that they would not reveal this to you unless it became necessary. When you were born, Everett, Lily, and Reece were right there in the room with me. As soon as the nurse handed you to my mom, Lily, I knew we had made the right decision. I watched all the love that was held by Lily and Reece pour from their hearts into yours. You are named after me and your mother, as you well know.

We had made the right decision. Everett and I pursued college and eventually found our way back to each other. We do not have any other children. We married when we were twenty-four. I was seventeen when I became pregnant with you. We have been married for eighteen years. We have resided here in Vegas this entire time."

Lily observed Camryn taking in all that had just been revealed. Everett stood up. "Camryn, there has never been a day that we have not thought about the decision and about you, our daughter."

Camryn burst into tears. "I don't know whether to be upset that you did not raise me or to thank you for giving me the best life ever by sacrificing the most precious gift, the gift of life."

Camryn stood and motioned for Jesse to stand. "Barrett, I need to leave. I cannot do any more truths today."

Camryn looked at her birth parents. "I'm sorry, but I need to embrace all that has been revealed. I don't want to say anything that would hurt your feelings. You both did what you thought was the best for me. For that, I am grateful. I had the best parents in my Mom and Pop Pop. They gave me everything that I needed. Love."

Camryn looked at her birth father and smiled. "To be honest, I always wondered why my Mom and Pop Pop seemed a bit more up in age than the rest of my friends' parents."

Barrett stood and held the door open for Camryn. "I will call you tonight. It's going to be okay," he whispered.

Camryn knew her birth mother was feeling the same as her. Without hesitation, Camryn walked to her birth father, Everett, and hugged him. "Thank you for not leaving Lily." She then walked over to her birth mother. "Thank you for making the ultimate sacrifice for me."

Silence. There were no words.

Barrett turned to his employers. "Let me get her and Jesse back on the road, and I will return. I'm sure you have questions for me, too."

"The Uber will be waiting outside for you and Jesse. It will return you to the hotel. I will call you later." Barrett pushed the down button on the elevator. Reaching for Camryn's hand, he kissed her on the forehead. The elevator doors opened. "I know that took a lot out of you. You hold the key to my heart, Camryn."

Camryn and Jesse stepped in. The elevator doors began to close. Jesse looked at Barrett. If Barrett only knew what Jesse had already guessed. He turned to see Camryn looking at Barrett. The truth was obvious. Love was a very powerful emotion. One that had already been unlocked.

CHAPTER 20

Walking towards the conference room, Barrett knew there would be questions of his involvement in this switch and how Barrett put two and two together.

He could see them through the glass conference room door. They were both standing, waiting for Barrett. Barrett took a deep breath. He opened the door.

"Barrett, thank you," Everett began. "We have kept this secret because of our love for daughter. Lily and I did not make the decision lightly when we asked Lily's mom and dad to raise our baby girl. After Camryn was born, we saw the love reflected in their eyes. Our daughter would never want for anything."

Barrett nodded. Everett was a straightshooter. In the years of being Everett's Vice President of Marketing, Barrett knew he was a man of few words, and those few words were concise and to the point. No room for discussion was required or requested.

Lily walked over to Barrett. "I want you to know that Everett and I have never stopped thinking about our one and only child and wondering how she was doing. I knew my mother and father would provide what Everett and I could not at that time in our lives. We made a promise to my mom and dad that if something should happen, the truth would be revealed. There was no contact, so that the secret could remain safely locked away. Little did we know, you would be the one to turn the key and unlock love."

Barrett again nodded.

"Lily and Everett," Barrett began. "I am not here to question the whys. Your decision was based on what you knew would be best for your daughter. When I read and then re-read again, I was astounded that I had opened something so valuable. It was a simple act. The turn of a key. I not only turned the key to reveal your love lost, but I turned the key to reveal love found."

EPILOGUE

Poking his head through the doorway, Barrett smiled. She was gathering her laptop and the folder for the client meeting this morning. Adding both of them to Vegas Heat had been a good idea. It had been perceived as far-fetched at first. Both had continued their relationship as if nothing had happened. The only change was the venue.

"Camryn, is everything ready in the conference room for this morning's pitch?"

Camryn raised her eyebrows in question. "Of course, we go through this same routine every new client presentation, and I know the drill. You, Jesse, Mom, Dad, and even Chloe are double-checking me. There's no reason to be worried."

Barrett walked into Camryn's office and reached for her hands. "Stop. And we always do this before every new client presentation." Camryn blushed. "Quickly, before anyone sees and we become the talk around the water cooler."

"We are already the talk around the office and the water cooler. The day you walked in here, the change began," Barrett kissed her.

Without missing a beat after his kiss, which Barrett felt was earth-shattering, Camryn did not miss a beat.

"Can you believe they are getting married this weekend, sweetheart? I knew there was a connection that first meeting at the hotel."

"Yes, I am over-the-moon thrilled for Jesse and Chloe. However, will I be able to wait until this weekend? Oh, the agony of the wait," Barrett pulled her close to his chest.

Camryn looked up at Barrett. Grinning from ear to ear. "Stop it, now, you're just teasing me. You do realize what is coming up this weekend, too?"

"How can I forget? You won't let me forget, plus you are my personal calendar. Yes, I realize what this weekend is. On Sunday, it is our one-year anniversary of wedded bliss." Barrett kissed her again.

"And if I continue the path of what my lips want to do to you, we are going to be late to the meeting," Barrett commented with a smile.

Camryn looked at her husband. One year. One year had passed. 365 days with Barrett. 365 days getting to know her Mom and Dad.

Camryn picked up everything that she could hold and handed Barrett what she could not. He opened the door for her, and they began the walk side by side to the conference room.

Was it fate? Was it destiny? Camryn did not want to think about how both had changed her life.

With the turn of one key, two lives had been changed. Love had been unlocked.

DANA ROEHRIG

Dana was born and raised in Louisville, Kentucky, alongside his three brothers and five sisters. His parents were hard-working individuals. Dana's mother was a wife, mom, homemaker, and quite busy (as you can imagine) with managing the day-to-day activities surrounding the family. Dana's father was a machinist. He worked two jobs to support the family and to make ends meet. Being no stranger to this work ethic, Dana has worked at UPS for twenty years. Prior to UPS, Dana worked in the Exposition Trade Show Industry. Dana still resides in Louisville, Kentucky. He has been married to his wife for 38 years. They have two wonderful children.

DE DE COX

Kentucky Romance Author
The Day You Go from Romance Junkie to
 # 1 Best-Selling Kentucky Romance Author

de de began pursuing her dream of becoming a romance author at the age of 30. Born and raised on the farm in Rooster Run, Kentucky, de de was raised on the core values of the 3Cs (kindness, caring, and compassion). Throughout her young adulthood, de de volunteered in the community with her family, and specifically, her grandmother, Bea. Growing up in the country, romance novels were her escape to another world. de de knew that one day, her dream of writing a romance novel would come true. Fast forward to 2018, when de de picked the book back up that she had begun in her early 30s. As in life, circumstances and direction change the course, but never the ending goal. Learning the industry and working with her publisher, Beyond Global Publishing, God opened many doors and many connections, and de de has never looked back.

de de became a published Kentucky romance author in 2018. She is the #1 best-selling Kentucky romance author of the Two Degrees Series, which features her son, Bo, as the male model. Little did de de know that her child would become the next FabiBo.

de de has now completed nine romance books and the tenth one is ready to debut, *Unlocking Love – Two Lives Changed by One Turn* debuting May 2023. She has received numerous Amazon bestseller rankings for her romance books.

de de has served as a board member of The Dream Factory of Louisville, Kentucky, Opal's Dream Foundation, Spalding University– Athletic Board, as well as volunteered with other charitable entities. de de received the coveted 2018 Spirit of Louisville Foundation - WLKY Bell Award for her volunteerism within her community and now serves on the board as trustee.

de de is active within the pageant industry. She is the co-director of the Miss Hillview, Miss Buttermilk, Miss Bullitt Blast Festival, and Miss Rolling Fork Iron Horse Festival prelims (Kentucky State Festival).

de de is employed as a medical malpractice paralegal with the elite law firm of Dolt, Thompson, Shepherd & Conway, PSC.

FAMILY (family always mean I love you), and this is true in de de's life. So many kind-hearted folks have traveled the journey. She has been married over 35 years to her best friend, Scott, from high school. She has two sons and one rescued fur baby.

de de encourages others to live by HIS word – Acts 20:35.

www.ingramcontent.com/pod-product-compliance
Lightning Source LLC
LaVergne TN
LVHW011846060526
838200LV00054B/4185